Chemical Pollution

Prakash Vishnoi

ISBN: 978-93-5438-840-8

Published in India 2020 by

A brand of
One Point Six Technologies Pvt. Ltd.
123, Building J2, Shram Seva Premises,
Wadala Truck Terminal, Wadala (E)
Mumbai 400037, Maharashtra, INDIA
E connect@thepencilapp.com
W www.thepencilapp.com

DEDICATION

Pollution is the introduction of contaminants into the natural environment that cause adverse change. **Pollution** can take the form of chemical substances or energy, such as noise, heat or light. **Pollutants**, the components of **pollution**, can be either foreign substances/energies or naturally occurring contaminants.

ACKNOWLEDGMENTS

The organic chemical industry, in the space of half a century, has produced millions of tons of persistent carbon-based compounds which can now be found in every part of the globe and in the body fat of every living creature. These compounds can be either intentionally released products (such as DDT), or unintentionally released as industrial chemical by-products (such as the dioxin-like substances). The majority of the dioxins and furans that have been introduced into the environment have come about as a result of the

incineration of municipal and clinical waste, which contains high levels of halogenated compounds and heavy metals. Persistent organic pollutants (POPs) are lipophilic and difficult to metabolise, and therefore they bioconcentrate in the body over time and biomagnify up the food web.

CONTENTS

1. WHAT IS POLLUTION

- Pollution is the introduction of harmful substances or products into the environment
- Main types of pollution
  - Water Pollution
  - Air Pollution
  - Soil Pollution
  - Biological
  - Nuclear

2 . WATER POLLUTION

Water pollution happens when toxic substances enter water bodies such as lakes, rivers, oceans and so on, getting dissolved in them, lying suspended in the water or depositing on the bed. This degrades the quality of water.

Not only does this spell disaster for aquatic ecosystems, the pollutants also seep through and reach the groundwater, which might end up in our households as contaminated water we use in our daily activities, including drinking.

Causes of Water Pollution

- Factors that contribute to water pollution can be categorized into two different groups
  - Point sources
  - Non-point sources
- Point sources are the easiest to identify and control
- Non point sources are ambiguously defined and harder to

control Point Sources

- Some point sources of water pollution include
  - Factories
  - Sewage system
  - Power plants
  - Underground coalmines
  - Oil wells
- Are direct sources of water pollution and can be reduced and monitored

Example of a point source

3. NON POINT SOURCE

• The term non-point source encompasses a large range of sources such as: –

when rain or snow moves through the ground and picks up pollutants as it moves towards a major body of water

– the runoff of fertilizers from farm animals and crop land

– air pollutants getting washed or deposited to earth

– storm water drainage from lawns, parking lots, and streets

4. AGRICOUTURE RUN OFF

Agricultural Runoff is water from **farm** fields due to irrigation, rain, or melted snow that flows over the earth that can absorb into the ground, enter bodies of waters or evaporate.

5. KINDS OF WATER POLLUTION

- Inorganic Pollutants
- Organic Pollutants
- Biological Pollutants Inorganic Pollutants
- Pb in gasoline
- Radionuclides
- Phosphorus, nitrogen (Great Lakes) Inorganic Trace Contaminants-Mercury

—methyl Hg and dimethyl Hg in fish

— Minamata Bay, Japan, 1950's

–Lead

—toxicity has been known for a long time

– Tetraethyl lead

—anti-knock additive for gas, 19301966 Phosphates and Nitrates

- Phosphates

—mostly a result of sewage outflow and phosphate detergents

– Additional phosphate grows excess algae...oxygen depletion

- Nitrates

—sewage and fertilizers Organic Pollutants

- Three classes of compounds

– Pesticides and Herbicides

– Materials for common household and industrial use

– Materials for industrial use Pesticides

- Chlorinated hydrocarbons

– DDT, heptachlor, etc

—2-15 years

- Organophosphates

– Malathion, methyl parathion

—1-2 weeks

• Carbamates

– Carbaryl, maneb, aldicarb

—days to weeks

• Pyrethroids – Pemethrin, decamethrin

—days to weeksHerbicides

• Triazines —e.g. atrazine, paraquat (interfere with photosynthesis)

• Systemic

—phenoxy compounds, N compounds, Alar, glyphosate (create excess growth hormones)

• Soil sterilants trifluralin, dalapon (kill soil microorganisms) Chemicals responsible for water pollution

• Each year 700-800 new chemicals are produced

- 55 million tons of hazardous chemical wastes are produced in the US each year
- The 20 most abundant compounds in groundwater at industrial waste disposal sites include TCE, benzene, vinyl chloride...all are carcinogens, and also affect liver, brain, and nervous system
- Polychlorinated biphenyls- Byproducts of plastic, lubricant, rubber & Paper Industry.

6. AIR POLLUTION

Air pollution is a mixture of solid particles and gases in the **air**. Car emissions, chemicals from factories, dust, pollen and mold spores may be suspended as particles. Ozone, a gas, is a major part of **air pollution** in cities. When ozone forms **air pollution**, it's also called smog.

Causes of Air Pollution

- carbon dioxide

-Deforestation and fossil fuel burning

- Sulfur dioxide

-burning of sulfur containing compounds of fossil fuels.

- Chlorofluorocarbons (CFCs)

reduces the amount of ozone. CFCs come from

–the burning of plastic foam items

–leaking refrigerator equipment

–spray cans

- Hydrocarbons- from petrol engines
- NOx- from burning of fossil fuels
- Suspended particulate matter -

by diesel engines, thermal power plants

• Lead compounds

- from petrol engines Natural Air Pollutants

• Natural air pollutants can include:

– Smoke from wild fires

– Methane released from live stock

– Volcanic eruptions

Consequences of Air Pollution

• CO2 is a good transmitter of sunlight, but it also partially restricts infrared radiation going back from the earth into space, which produces the socalled greenhouse effect that prevents a drastic cooling of the Earth during the night

- Increasing the amount of CO_2 in the atmosphere reinforces this effect and is expected to result in a warming of the Earth's surface
- CO_2 in atmosphere GLOBAL WARMING

7. GREEN HOUSE EFFECT

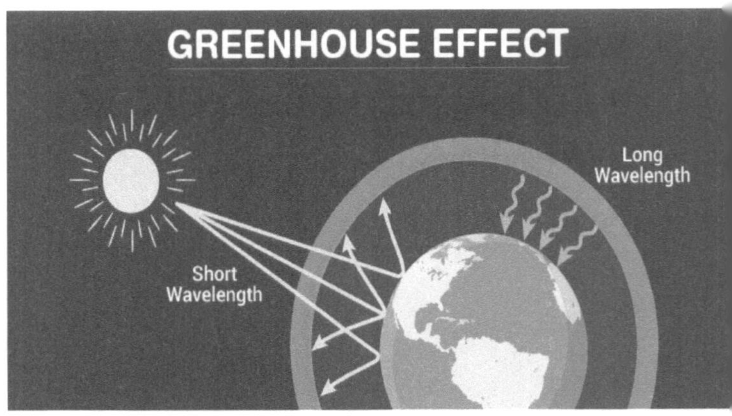

The greenhouse effect is the process by which radiation from a planet's atmosphere warms the planet's surface to a temperature above what it would be without this atmosphere. Radiatively active gases (i.e., greenhouse gases) in a planet's atmosphere radiate energy in all directions. Part of this radiation is directed towards the surface, warming it. The intensity of the downward radiation – that is, the strength of the greenhouse effect – will depend on the atmosphere's temperature and on the amount of greenhouse gases that the atmosphere contains.

8. A SMOGGY

Photochemical Smog

- Sulfur dioxide, nitrogen oxides, ozone and peroxyacl nitrates (PANs), give rise to photo chemical smog, irritates eyes and lungs.
- Chronic exposure of leaves and needles to air pollutants can also

break down the waxy coating that helps prevent excessive water loss and damage from diseases, pests, drought and frost

9. SOIL POLLUTION

Soil pollution refers to the contamination of soil with anomalous concentrations of toxic substances. It is a serious environmental concern since it harbours many health hazards. For example, exposure to soil containing high concentrations of benzene increases the risk of contracting leukaemia. An image detailing the discolouration of soil due to soil pollution is provided below.

Causes of Soil Pollution

- Contamination of soil system by considerable quantity of chemicals or other substances resulting in reduction of its fertility.
- Four Main causes of Soil pollution
  – Construction
  – Agriculture
  – Domestic waste
  – Industrial Waste Chemicals causing soil pollution
- Metallic pollutants- textiles, dyes, soaps, detergents, drugs, cement,

rubber, paper, metal industries release Fe, Pb, Cu, Zn, Hg, Cd, CN, acids, alkalies etc.

- Agro chemicals- Fertilizers, pesticides, insecticides, weedicides, rodenticides, fumigants release toxic chemicals like Pb, As, Cd, Hg, Co etc.
- Radioactive Chemicals Biological Pollution
- Disturbance of the ecological balance by the accidental or deliberate introduction of a foreign organism, animal or plant species into an environment.
- an individual organism (internal biological pollution by parasites or pathogens)
- A population (by genetic change) continued

- a community
- a habitat (by modification of physicalchemical conditions),
- An ecosystem (by alteration of energy and organic material flow).
- Biopollution may also cause decline in naturalness of nature conservation areas. Biological Agents
- Soil gets human, animal & bird excreta
- Digested sewage sludge
- Heavy applications of manure to soil Scale of Biologic Contaminant Problem: - Major cause of infant deaths in third world -Diarrhea kills 4-15 million children/year - Bacteria, viruses, parasites Radiological & Nuclear pollution
- Special form of physical pollution

of air, water and soil with radioactive materials.

- Radioactivity- Property of certain elements like Ra, Th, U etc to spontaneously emit alpha, beta & gamma rays by disintegration of atomic nuclei. Sources
- Nuclear explosions and detonations of nuclear weapons – U-235, Pu-239 for fission, H & Li for fusion. Fallouts contain Sr-90, Cs-137, I-131
- Defense weapon production- C-14, I125, P-32
- Nuclear waste handling and disposalhigh level & low level Sources
- Mining – radioactive gases like radon
- Nuclear accidents

- Medical X-Rays- from diagnostic X-rays & radiation therapy for cancer.
- Nuclear reactors- U-235, U-238, Th-232 Effects of nuclear pollution
- The effects vary from organism to organism and from level of radioactivity of nuclear isotopes. The radiations destroy the cells in human body and causes cancer.
- A longer exposure to radioactive radiations can damage the DNA cells that results in cancer, genetic defects for the generations to come and even death. continued
- Kills foetus in the womb
- Affects animals, some species preferentially accumulate specific radioactive materials- oysters deposit Zn65, fish Fe-55, marine

animals Sr-90. Chemical Warfare agents

- A chemical used in warfare is called a chemical warfare agent (CWA).
- These agents may be in liquid, gas or solid form. Liquid agents are generally designed to evaporate quickly; such liquids are said to be volatile or have a high vapour pressure.
- In July 1917, the Germans employed mustard gas. Mustard gas easily penetrates leather and fabric to inflict painful burns on the skin.
- Chemical warfare agents are divided into lethal and incapacitating categories. A substance is classified as

incapacitating if less than 1/100 of the lethal dose causes incapacitation, e.g., through nausea or visual problems.

- Choking Agents (e.g., phosgene, chlorine)
- Blister Agents (e.g., nitrogen mustard, Lewisite)
- Nerve Agents (e.g., tabun, sarin, VX)
- The most commonly used chemicals are four lungdestroying poisons: chlorine, chloropicrin, phosgene, and trichloromethyl chloroformate, along with a skin-blistering agent known as mustard gas, or bis (2chloroethyl) sulfide.

10.AIR POLLUTION IN INDIA

Today, air pollution has emerged as a global public health problem and is identified as a major environmental health hazard by agencies such as the World Health Organization (WHO) and governments around the world. An increase in concentration of pollutants - both gaseous and solid - is among the largest health risk in the world and according to the latest data released by WHO, indoor and outdoor air pollution were responsible for 3.7 million deaths of people aged under 60 in 2012. In recent years, air pollution has acquired critical dimensions and the air quality in most Indian cities that monitor outdoor air pollution fail to meet WHO guidelines for safe levels. The levels of PM2.5 and PM10 (Airborne particles smaller than 2.5 micrometers in diameter and 10 micrometers in diameter) as well as concentration of dangerous carcinogenic substances such as Sulphur Dioxide (SO2) and Nitrogen Dioxide (NO2) have reached alarming proportions in most Indian cities, putting people at additional risk of respiratory diseases and other health problems. Furthermore, the issue of indoor air pollution has put women and children at high risk.

Impact of air pollution in india

Air pollution, both indoor (household) and outdoor, has had a significant impact on the health of citizens as well as the economy. The adverse effects of air pollution are not just restricted to the urban areas but also impact rural areas, where a majority of the population relies on kerosene and burning of biomass for lighting and cooking purposes respectively.

Air pollution is among the leading causes of death in India

The Global Burden of Disease Report has ranked outdoor air pollution as the fifth leading cause of death in India and indoor air pollution as the third leading cause. Outdoor air pollution was responsible for 6,20,000 deaths in 2010, increasing six-fold from 1,00,000 deaths in 2000. Moreover, a research study by researchers at the University of Chicago, Harvard and Yale estimated that high Particulate Matter (PM) concentration is responsible for reducing the life expectancy by 3.2

years for 660 million Indians living in urban conglomerates.

Negative impact on agricultural productivity

A recent research study "Recent climate and air pollution impacts on Indian agriculture" by scientists at the University of California, San Diego suggests the adverse impact of air pollution caused by Short-Lived Climate Pollutants (SLCPs) on agricultural productivity. They observed that the yield of wheat in 2010 has reduced by almost 36% and that of rice by 20% when compared to figures from 1980, negating for climate change. SLCPs such as ozone and black carbon are released into the atmosphere by motor vehicle exhausts and rural cook stoves respectively. These SLCPs remain in the atmosphere for short periods.

Cost of Air pollution amounts to 3% of the GDP

A World Bank report titled 'Diagnostic Assessment of Select Environmental Challenges in India" highlighted that the annual cost of air pollution, specifically pollution from particulate matter (burning of fossil fuels) amounts to 3% of the GDP of the country; outdoor air pollution accounting for 1.7% and indoor air pollution for 1.3%. The report also observed that a 30% reduction in particulate emissions by 2030 would save India $105 billion in health-related costs; a 10% reduction would save $24 billion. In light of the adverse impacts, coupled with the fact that the concentration of particulate matter in 180 Indian cities is almost six times higher than the standards set by the WHO, the issue of quality of air has become a major concern for the government of India.

Summary of key Government Initiatives & Policy Measures to tackle

the issue

Amid growing concerns pertaining to rising air pollution, government of India has taken various initiatives as well as introduced policies to address the issue. In order to prevent and control air pollution, the Parliament of India enacted the Air (Prevention and Control of Pollution) Act, 1981 on 29th March 1981, which came into force on the 15th May of the same year. The Central Pollution Control Board (CPCB), a statutory organization under the Ministry of Environment & Forests (MoEF) has been entrusted with the responsibility of ensuring ambient air quality and has been conferred and assigned the power and functions to achieve the stipulated objective. Thereby, the CPCB in association with various State Pollution Control Boards (SPCBs) monitors the ambient air quality according to the National Ambient Air Quality Standards (NAAQS) with the help of 580 manual stations established in 244 cities, towns and industrial areas. . Steps to curb vehicular emission With the increase in number of vehicles on Indian roads, air pollution resulting from vehicular emissions has become the main source of air pollution in the urban centres of the country. Moreover, in FY 2014, the share of diesel cars in overall car sales was

53%. According to a report released by the International Council on Clean Transportation, diesel vehicles are responsible for 56% of all PM emissions and 70% of all Nitrogen Oxides (NOx) emissions from on-road vehicles in India. Moreover, the content of sulphur in fuel makes it dirtier and lowers the efficiency of catalytic convertors, which control emissions in automobiles. Therefore, several steps have been taken to mitigate the issue of vehicular emissions.

Adopting emission norms and fuel regulation

standards

Since the year 2000, India started adopting European emission and fuel regulations for all categories of vehicles. Under this plan,the Bharat Stage II emission standards were introduced initially in the four metro cities to manage the amount of air pollutants released by the internal combustion engine equipments by using cleaner fuel with low sulphur content and improved combustion engines. Accordingly, oil marketing companies were required to supply BS compliant fuel and auto manufacturers had to upgrade engines in a phased manner. Later on, the Bharat Stage fuel norms were applied to the rest of the country; as of 26th November 2011, BS – IV norms are applicable in 34 cities whereas BS –III norms are applicable in the rest of the country. However, India has been following European norms with a time lag of five years and it is infact a decade behind developing countries such as Turkey and Brazil in introducing cleaner-burning fuel. The Saumitra Chaudhari Committee, formed to look into automobile fuel emission standards, has recommended that the government introduce the Bharat Stage – V norms across the country by 2020.

11. ENVIRONMENTAL RISK ANALYSIS

Risk analysis allows us to estimate impacts on the environment and on human health when we have not measured or cannot measure or directly observe those impacts. It also lets us compare these impacts. In this chapter, we introduce the concept of risk analysis and risk management. The former is the measurement and comparison of various forms of risk; the latter involves the techniques used to reduce these risks.

RISKS

Most pollution control and environmental laws were enacted in the early 1970s in order to protect public health and welfare. 1 In these laws and throughout this text, a substance is considered a pollutant if it has been perceived to have an adverse effect on human health. In recent years, increasing numbers of sub- stances appear to pose such threats; the Clean Air Act listed seven hazardous substances between 1970 and 1989, and now lists approximately 300! The en- vironmental engineer thus has an additional job: to help determine the comparative risks from various environmental pollutants and, further, to determine which risks are most important to decrease or eliminate. Adverse effects on human health are sometimes difficult to identify and to determine. Even when such an adverse effect has been identified, it is still diffi- cult to recognize those components of the individual's environment that are associated with it. Risk analysts refer to these components as risk factors. In general, a risk factor should meet the following conditions:

- Exposure to the risk factor precedes appearance of the adverse effect.
- The risk factor and the adverse effect are consistently associated.

That is, the adverse effect is not usually observed in the absence of the risk factor.

• The more of the risk factor there is, or the greater its intensity, the greater the adverse effect, although the functional relationship need not be linear or monotonic

• The occurrence or magnitude of the adverse effect is statistically signifi- cantly greater in the presence of the risk factor than in its absence. Identification of a risk factor for a particular adverse effect may be made with confidence only if the relationship is consonant with, and does not contradict, existing knowledge of the cellular and organismic mechanisms producing the adverse effect. Identification of the risk factor is more difficult than identification of an ad- verse effect. For example, we are now certain that cigarette smoke is unhealthy, both to the smokermprimary smoke riskmand to those around the smokerm secondary smoke risk. Specifically, lung cancer, chronic obstructive pulmonary disease, and heart disease occur much more frequently among habitual smokers than among nonsmokers or even in the whole population including smokers. The increased frequency of occurrence of these diseases is statistically significant. Cigarette smoke is thus a risk factor for these diseases;

smokers and people ex- posed to secondhand smoke are at increased risk for them. Notice, however, that we do not say that cigarette smoking causes lung cancer, chronic obstructive pulmonary disease, or heart disease, because we have not identified the actual causes, or etiology, of any of them. How, then, has cigarette smoking been identified as a risk factor if it cannot be identified as the cause? This observation about cigarette smoke was not made, and indeed could not be made, until the middle of the twentieth century, when the lifespan in at least the devel- oped countries of the world was long enough to observe the diseases that had been correlated with exposure to cigarette smoke. In the first half of the twentieth century, infectious diseases were a primary cause of death. With the advent of antibiotics and the ability to treat such diseases, the lifespan in the developed nations of the world lengthened, and cancer and heart disease became the lead- ing causes of death. From the early 1960s, when the average lifespan in the United States was about 70, lifelong habitual cigarette smokers were observed to die from lung cancer at ages between 55 and 65. This observation, which associated early death with cigarette smoke, identified cigarette smoke as a risk factor.

12. RADIOACTIVE WASTE

This chapter presents a general background discussion of the interaction of ion- izing radiation with matter, as well as a discussion of the environmental effects of nuclear generation of electricity and of radionuclides that are in the accessi- ble environment. The chapter focuses on radioactive waste as an environmen- tal pollutant, discusses the impact of ionizing radiation on environmental and public health, and summarizes options available today for the management and disposal of radioactive waste.

RADIATION

X-rays were discovered by Wilhelm Roentgen in 1895. The following year Henri Becquerel observed radiation similar to x-rays emanating from certain uranium salts. In 1898, Marie and Pierre Curie studied radiation from two ura- nium ores, pitchblende and chalcolite, and isolated two additional elements that exhibited radiation similar to uranium but considerably stronger. These two el- ements were named radium and polonium. The discovery and isolation of these radioactive elements marks the beginning of the "atomic age." The Curies classified the radiation from radium and polonium into three types, according to the direction of deflection in a magnetic field. These three types of radiation were called alpha (~), beta (]3), and gamma (y). Becquerel's observation correlated gamma radiation with Roentgen's x-rays. In 1905, Ernest Rutherford identified alpha particles emanating from uranium as ionized helium atoms, and in 1932 Sir James Chadwick characterized as neutrons the highly penetrating radiation that results when beryllium is bombarded with alpha particles. Modern physics has subsequently identified other subatomic particles, including positrons, muons, and pions, but not all of these are of equal concern. Management of radioactive waste requires an understanding of the sources and effects of alpha, beta, gamma, and neutron emissions.

13. SOLID WASTE

Solid wastes other than hazardous and radioactive materials are considered in this chapter. Such solid wastes are often called municipal solid waste (MSW) and consist of all the solid and semisolid materials discarded by a community. The fraction of MSW produced in domestic households is called refuse. The compo- sition of refuse has been changing over the past decades. Much of the material historically has been food wastes, but new materials such as plastics and alu- minum cans have been added to refuse, and the use of kitchen garbage grinders has decreased the food waste component. Most of the 2000 new products cre- ated each year by American industry eventually find their way into MSW and contribute to individual disposal problems. The components of refuse are garbage, or food wastes; rubbish, including glass, tin cans, and paper; and trash, including larger items like tree limbs, old appliances, pallets, and so forth, that are not usually deposited in garbage cans. The relationship between solid waste and human disease is intuitively obvious but difficult to prove. If a rat is sustained by an open dump, and that rat sus- tains a flea that transmits murine typhus to a human, the absolute proof of the pathway requires finding the particular rat and fleaman obviously impossible task. Nonetheless, we have observed more than twenty human diseases that are associated with solid waste disposal sites, and there is little doubt that improper solid waste disposal is a health hazard. Disease vectors are the means by which disease organisms are transmitted, such as water, air, and food. The two most important disease vectors related to solid waste are rats and flies. Flies are such prolific breeders that 70,000 flies can be produced in i ft 3 of garbage, and they carry many diseases like bacillary dysentery. Rats not only destroy property and infect by direct bite, but carry insects like fleas and ticks that may also act as vectors. The plagues of the Middle Ages were directly associated with the rat populations. Public health is also threatened by infiltration of leachate from MSW disposal into groundwater, particularly drinking water supplies. Leachate is formed when rainwater collects in landfills, pits, waste ponds, or waste lagoons, and stays in contact with waste material long enough to leach out and dissolve some of its chemical and biochemical constituents. Leachate may be a major groundwater and surface water contaminant, particularly where there is heavy rainfall and rapid percolation through the soil.

QUANTITIES AND CHARACTERISTICS OF MUNICIPAL SOLID WASTE

The quantities of MSW generated in a community may be estimated by one of three techniques: input analysis, secondary data analysis, and output analysis. Input analysis estimates MSW based on use of a number of products. For exam- ple, if 100,000 cans of beer are sold each week in a particular community, the MSW, including litter, might be expected to include

100,000 aluminum cans per week. But obtaining waste characteristics' data from such information is often dif- ficult and inaccurate. When possible, solid waste generation should be measured by output analysis--that is, by weighing the refuse deposited at the disposal site. Refuse must generally be weighed in any case, because fees for use of the facil- ity (called tipping fees) depend on the weight of the refuse. Daily weight of refuse varies with the day of the week and the week of the year. Weather conditions also affect refuse weight, since moisture content can vary widely depending on how much rainwater enters the waste. If every truckload cannot be weighed, statisti- cal methods must be used to estimate the total quantity from sample truckload weights

Characteristics of Municipal Solid Waste

Refuse management depends on both the characteristics of the site and the characteristics of the MSW itself: gross composition, moisture content, particle size, chemical composition, and density. Gross composition may be the most important characteristic affecting MSW disposal, or the recovery of materials and energy from refuse. Composition varies from one community to another, as well as with time in any one commu- nity. Refuse composition is expressed "as generated" or "as disposed," since moisture transfer takes place during the disposal process and thereby changes the weights of the various fractions of refuse. Table 12-1 shows typical components of average U.S. refuse. The numbers in the table are useful only as guidelines, as each community has characteristics that influence its solid waste production and composition.

ABOUT THE AUTHOR

1. *I AM PRAKASH VISHNOI FROM JODHPUR, RAJASTHAN*
2. *I AM STUDENT*
3. *MY BIRTH PLACE IS JODHPUR*

www.ingramcontent.com/pod-product-compliance
Lightning Source LLC
LaVergne TN
LVHW050422160726
843469LV00041B/1190

* 9 7 8 9 3 5 4 3 8 8 4 0 8 *